The Class Champion

Written by A. M. Dassu

Illustrated by Sibu Puthenveettil

Collins

Chapter 1

Ms Young pointed at the whiteboard. "Competition time!"
Everyone whispered excitedly to the person beside them.
"I want you all to make a 3-D animal habitat and bring it in
on Monday. It can be *any* animal, but it would be brilliant
if you linked it to this term's India topic." She looked
at us through her glasses to check we were listening.
"The habitat can be any shape or size, but it should
show all the things that the animal you've chosen needs
to survive. Do you understand?"

3D Animal Habitat
Competition

"Yessss," said Sam to Hetal as the bell rang. "This is
going to be SO easy."

I sighed. Sam would win – again. Ms Young always gave
her bonus house points. Her work was always the best.
Sam had all this amazing craft material. And her mum was
home after school and at weekends to help Sam, unlike my
parents who had to work different shifts.

"Oh! Class 4Y, stop!" Ms Young shouted, as we rushed to grab our coats.

I froze mid-step.

"I forgot to say, there's a special prize for the *best* habitat … I can't go to the football game next month, so I've decided to give the winner my TWO tickets!"

OK, I *had* to win now. But how would I beat Sam? She had EVERYTHING and was the smartest kid in the class. It would be so unfair if she won – she already had a season ticket.

I needed to win. Somehow.

Chapter 2

"Here you go," said Mum, as she placed a plate of grilled chicken and chips in front of me. "I have to leave for work now, but I'll be home tomorrow. We can spend some time together then, OK?" She kissed the top of my head and grabbed her hospital badge which was dangling off the back of a chair.

"Thanks," I said, picking up my fork.

"Why the face?" asked Mum. "Dad will be back from his last delivery slot in an hour. And your gran is popping in with his food now … love you!"

I didn't say anything as Mum walked out of the kitchen. I couldn't tell her that I didn't want to wait all day till she woke up from her night shift to start on my project. And Dad had been up since 4 o'clock this morning, so I couldn't ask him to help. *I'll just have to make the best habitat myself*, I thought, as I shovelled bits of chicken into my mouth.

The doorbell rang.

"Phew, you're here," Mum said, sounding relieved. "I'm running late!"

The front door clicked shut.

"Mustafa! It's Nani!"

She burst in with a waft of lamb and rice, holding a small silver saucepan.

"Oh no! You've already eaten!" Nani's smiley
face dropped.

"Sorry, Nani. I was really hungry and Mum made
me this."

"That's OK, my little moon," she said, putting
the saucepan on the hob. "You can have the leftovers
for lunch tomorrow." Nani's eyes searched the room.
"Where's the used wrapping paper your mum mentioned?"

"I haven't seen it," I said, shrugging.

"Can you find it for me? It's urgent."

9

I pushed my chair back and stood up. *Ugh!* I didn't have time to hunt for bits of used wrapping paper. I needed to work on my project to win those football tickets! That was more urgent.

"I want to revive the old books I found in my attic with it," Nani added, as she took my empty plate to the sink.

I blew out a long breath before rushing out of the kitchen. Nani had a drawer FULL of used foil, which she'd made *me* smooth out, and now she wanted crinkly old birthday wrap. I huffed into the living room. Everything was in its place. No old rubbish. Mum binned everything. She was the exact opposite of Nani, who stored things "for a rainy day".

I finally found the wrapping paper in the downstairs cupboard, just as Dad arrived home. Nani left and I started working on my project. It was time to make a plan.
I decided I'd make a tiger's habitat. They were my favourite animals in the whole world *and* they lived in India, so it was perfect.

I drew a 2-D plan of the habitat, including where
I'd put the water and trees, then leant back in my chair.
I couldn't help but think about all the art equipment Sam
always bragged about. *She's probably painting on her
easel and printing the whole habitat off on her 3-D printer,*
I thought. *We don't even have a* normal *printer*! I was
having to use lined paper. We didn't even have any card, or
coloured paper.

I groaned. There was no way I'd beat Sam. I'd be better off watching TV with Dad. I tucked my chair in, opened the door to the living room and sighed. Dad was snoring away on the sofa.

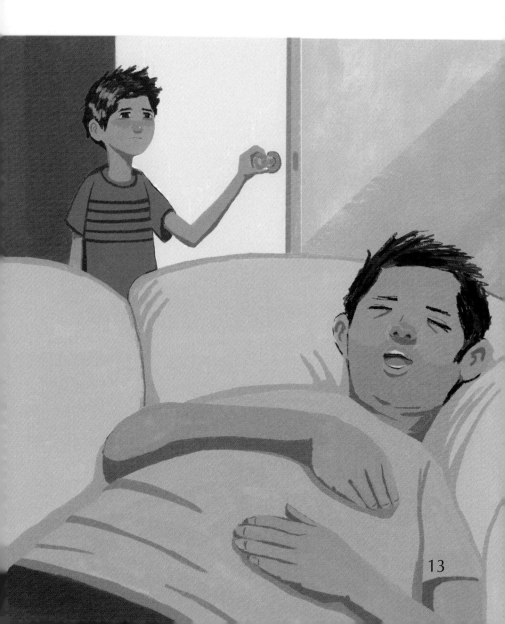

Chapter 3

The next morning, I jumped out of bed as if I
was late for school. I'd had a dream about going to
the football match. I couldn't give up on the project yet.
I had to do my best to win, even if it meant spending all
of Saturday working on it.

Mum was asleep after her night shift and Dad was at
work, so it wasn't like I had anything better to do.

I quietly grabbed Mum's old illustrated encyclopedia
from my bookshelf – making sure I didn't disturb her.
Nani had given it to me last year. She'd kept it all this time.
It was over 20 years old, but it was still pretty cool. I started
off by tracing over a tiger, then drew over the lines to make
it look like I'd sketched it.

I did my best colouring in, going over the black with my pencil where the colour of my felt tip was running out. I told myself it looked fine – more natural. I couldn't ask Mum to buy me new felt tips right now and I needed to get it done before Monday.

We did have plenty of PVA glue though, so once I'd cut out the tiger, green trees and grass I'd drawn, I stuck them all inside the 3-D paper box I'd made.

I was finishing off a packet of cheese and onion crisps when Mum walked sleepily into the kitchen, still in her pyjamas.

"Look, Mum," I said proudly. "Do you think it will win?"

"Wow, Mustafa!" said Mum, reaching towards the table to pick it up.

"Mum, don't!"

I grabbed her arm before she touched a paper wall
and it all collapsed.

"I've just finished gluing it together – it's still wet."

"Oops! Sorry!" Mum smiled. "Is this what you've been
doing all day?"

"Yeah," I said, staring at my socks, hoping she liked it.

"You're very talented! Look at that tiger! How can that
not win?" She wrapped her arms around me.

"Can I leave it next to the radiator to dry properly overnight?" I asked, as Mum filled the kettle with water.

"Yes, of course," she said. "I'll make sure we all stay away from it."

Chapter 4

I smiled as I got dressed the next morning. I had a whole day with the TV all to myself.

I raced downstairs and poked my head into the living room.

"Mum?" I said.

"Ah, Mustafa, you're up," said Dad, putting his mug on the coffee table. "Mum's gone to work and I'm just heading outside. What's your plan for the day?"

"Erm … to watch cartoons."

Dad laughed and ruffled my hair. "As it's Sunday, I'll allow it." He picked up his chainsaw and toolbox, then opened the patio door. "I'll be chopping down the overgrown fir tree at the bottom of the garden, OK?"

"OK," I said.

"Be good!"

The patio door slammed. The house fell silent. The only sound now was the washing machine rumbling in the kitchen.

My stomach groaned. *What shall I eat?* I asked myself, walking into the kitchen towards the cereal cupboard. The smell of coffee still lingered from Dad's breakfast.

SQUELCH.

My socks felt wet.

SQUELCH.

My socks *were* wet. I looked down. I was standing in a shallow pool of water.

The water was oozing from the washing machine. It had leaked again.

Oh no ... the washing machine was next to the radiator ... where I'd left my project.

The whole 3D tiger habitat had collapsed.

"NO!" I screamed. I sat on the wet floor, unable to stop my tears. I brought my knees to my chest and cried – more than I'd cried about anything before. I wanted those tickets so badly. *Why did I even bother?* I thought. I wasn't going to win anyway.

When it felt like my eyes had no tears left, I looked up.
I needed to bin the soaked project and dry the floor.
Mum wouldn't be happy if the water got into the hallway
and ruined the carpet.

I used a whole kitchen roll to wipe the floor, and then
gathered my project – now just bits of soggy paper – into
a black bin bag.

I opened the front door to put the bag in the bin, and a familiar face rode past on a bike. It was Sam.

I froze as if I was facing a tiger.

"Oh, you live here?" she asked, stopping with one hand on her handlebar. "Have you made your habitat?"

"Erm …" I eyed the bin bag.

But she continued before I could answer.

"My mum bought me cute miniature animals for my habitat. I think I used every single plastic brick I have! It's huge!" Sam sat with her shoulders back, as if she'd already won.

I looked at her, my mind blank. I didn't know what to say.

"What are you going to bring in? That bag of rubbish?" She pointed to the black bag dangling from my hands.

How did she know? I tried to keep my face still, even though it felt as if she'd hit me in my stomach.

Sam giggled and rode off, leaving me standing with my rubbish.

Chapter 5

I ended up watching so much TV my eyes felt square. It was the only thing that distracted me from thinking about losing the class competition.

The phone rang, forcing me to get up.

It was Nani. "Have you eaten, my little moon?" she asked.

"Yes, Nani. Dad made me a kebab roll."

"That's good … Oh, Mustafa, tell me, did your dad bring any cardboard home for me from work? I'll come and pick it up."

PING!

A light switched on in
my brain.

Nani was so annoying, keeping and reusing
EVERYTHING, but it might be a good thing for *me*!

"Mustafa?" Nani asked, because I hadn't replied.

"I'll ask him in a minute," I said. "Are you busy, Nani?
Can I come round, please? I'll bring the cardboard. I need
your help with something."

"Of course!" Nani sounded surprised. "I'd love for you to come. You can help me finish off making these samosas."

Ugh, I thought. I didn't have time for that! But if that's what it would take to get a new habitat made, I was willing to do anything, even help fill samosas.

Chapter 6

Nani stared at me for a long time after I'd finished
explaining what a tiger's habitat needed to have.
The samosa she'd just filled and folded into a triangle was
still in her hand. Had she even listened?

"OK, you pack these into this tub," she said, pointing at
the freshly filled samosas arranged on a tray. "I'll go and see
what I can find."

After I'd clicked the tub's lid shut, I ran upstairs
to find Nani. She was darting out of her room into
the spare bedroom.

"Ah, come, Mustafa. I've found lots of things we
can use."

I followed her inside and copied her as she sat down cross-legged on a plastic mat.

In between us were colourful spools of thread, different-sized buttons, empty jam jars, string, ribbons, pieces of fabric, plastic jewels and lots of scattered sequins.

"Wow!" I said.

Nani smiled. "Grab that piece of cardboard."
She pointed at a thick large piece of cardboard leaning
against the wall and gestured for me to put it on the floor.

"Shall we cover this with some silky fabric?"

"Yes!" I squealed. I bet Sam didn't have anything
like this!

I grabbed an emerald green piece that I recognised
from one of Nani's old suits and wrapped it around
the cardboard. Nani stapled it in place.

We started off working quietly. I drew and cut out
a tiger, while Nani picked out black and orange sequins for
me to stick on for stripes.

"I'm so happy you came, Mustafa," she said, handing
me a black sequin to glue down. "I used to love spending
my days with you. I'd pick you up from nursery every day.
Do you remember?"

"I do, Nani. I remember eating jam sandwiches in the park with you."

She beamed and I smiled back, glad I'd made her happy.

"What do you think we could use this for?" asked Nani, picking up a glass jar.

"Maybe we could stack them to create an old building?"

"Great idea, Mustafa! We could make them into turrets for the maharaja's palace ruins in the background!" Nani's eyes sparkled. "Every Indian tiger should live with one nearby – the perfect place to shelter." She pulled my chin to look at her smiling face and added, "We can fill them with coloured water! I can make liquid saffron in the kitchen for red, and turmeric for yellow. They'll look magical!"

I grinned, imagining it. Nani was amazingly creative.
My stomach did an excited somersault. I couldn't wait till
Sam saw this. It would beat her dumb habitat any day.

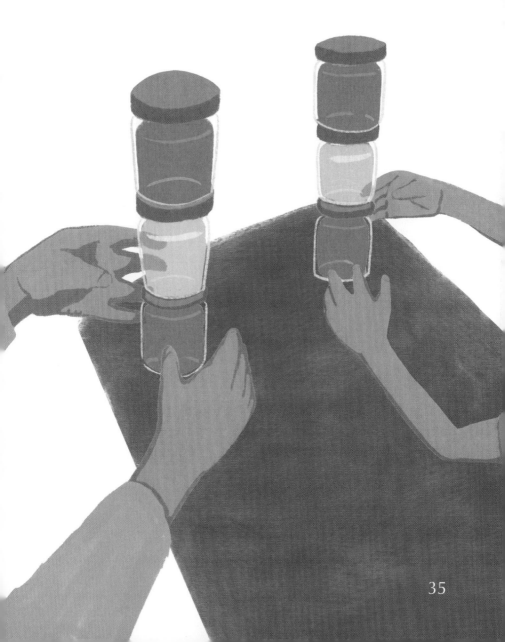

Chapter 7

We worked nonstop. Nani wrapped emerald green
and gold ribbons around old kitchen roll tubes for the trees.
I folded and stuck bits of white string down as ripples in
the enormous swamp flowing through the middle.

"You've got so many cool things, Nani."

"I've learnt to keep everything, Mustafa. My siblings
and I grew up extremely poor. I washed all our clothes
by hand, tutored other kids to make money and we
walked *everywhere*. We even used old drink cans
for footballs. Everything is useful to you when you don't
have much."

I looked at her as I never had before. Now I could understand why Nani saved everything – these things were like precious jewels to her.

"I always taught your mum that you never know when something will come in handy. And now I'm showing you too." Nani took some plastic gems that had dropped off her old clothes and fixed them to the leaves made of green ribbon. "Flowers," she said.

I smiled. I felt guilty now that I'd complained about the old things she wanted.

The phone rang and Nani got up to answer it while I stood back with my hands on my hips to admire the habitat. It was impressively big and bright.

I tried to lift it to take it downstairs but couldn't – it was too heavy! I swallowed, my throat suddenly tight. I'd never get it to school without a car and people to help me, and I wouldn't have any of those tomorrow morning.

My heart felt as heavy as the habitat. All our work had been wasted. I wouldn't even have a chance of winning now.

Chapter 8

At school the next day, I tried to keep a straight face and not show how miserable I felt as I watched everyone else putting their habitats on display. Theirs were all made with the usual shop-bought card and photo printouts, and coloured with glitter and gel pens. *Mine is so much better*, I thought. This just wasn't fair.

Sam charged through the door with her plastic brick construction, a smug look on her face. "Oh look! Mine's the biggest!" she said, as she put it down.

Mine was even bigger. But she'd never know.

I didn't feel like playing with anyone at lunchtime, so I sat on a bench watching the others kick a ball around. When the bell rang, I was first into the classroom.

I gasped out loud.

How did it get here?

My habitat was displayed in the middle of everyone's!

"Mustafa!" said Ms Young from her desk. "Your gran brought in your habitat half an hour ago. She managed to find someone to give her a lift to school and help her drop it off."

Nani really was the best! I sat down at my table, grinning as everyone came in and stared at it.

When Sam saw it, she stopped. Her cheeks turned as red as tomatoes, then she marched to her table.

It wasn't until five minutes before the bell rang that
Ms Young said, "Right, Class 4Y. Time to announce
the winner. It's been a really difficult decision to make …"
Could it be me? I wondered.
"And it's clear that some of you had considerable help …"

I gulped. She meant me. Nani had just delivered my
project for me. *Oh no!* I could hear my heart beating like
a drum. It was going to be Sam … it always was.

"The competition champion is …"

I slouched and looked down.

"… drum roll … Mustafa! I was so impressed with your inventive use of recycled materials!"

My mouth fell open but I couldn't move.

"Mustafa, you won!" Serena nudged me.

I sat up. It was true! This wasn't a dream!

"Well done, Mustafa!" said Ms Young, walking towards my table. "It really is incredible. It must have taken you ages to make."

A chair scraped back. The whole class turned to see Sam stomping off furiously towards the door.

"Who will you take to the football with you?" asked Ms Young.

I didn't need to think about it. "My nani!" I said.

Mustafa's determination

interest

focus

pride

panic

dejection

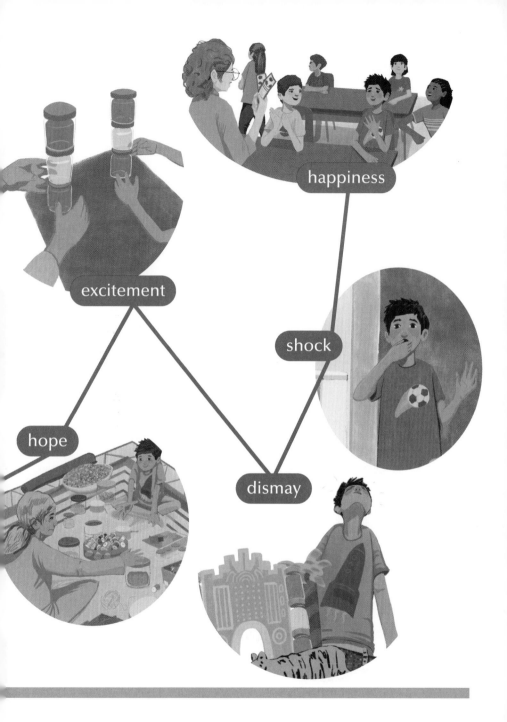

happiness

excitement

shock

hope

dismay

 Ideas for reading

Written by Gill Matthews
Primary Literacy Consultant

Reading objectives:

- draw inferences such as inferring characters' feelings, thoughts and motives from their actions, and justifying inferences with evidence
- identify how language, structure and presentation contribute to meaning
- participate in discussion about books, taking turns and listening to what others say

Spoken language objectives:

- articulate and justify answers, arguments and opinions
- use spoken language to develop understanding through speculating, hypothesising, imagining and exploring ideas
- participate in discussions, presentations, performances, role play, improvisations and debates

Curriculum links: Science – Living things and their habitats; Relationships Education – Families and people who care for me

Interest words: charged, marched, stomping

Build a context for reading

- Ask children to look closely at the front cover illustration and describe what they can see. Ask what they think the boy at the bottom of the picture is doing. Discuss the title and ask the children what it means to them.
- Read the back-cover blurb. Ask children if they think Mustafa will be the class champion in the end.
- Discuss what the children think they have learnt about Mustafa so far.

Understand and apply reading strategies

- Read pp2–5 aloud to the children. Ask what more they have learnt about Mustafa and how they feel about Sam. Ask them to describe what the class challenge is.
- Ask children to read Chapter 2. Explore how they would describe Mustafa. Encourage them to refer to the text to justify their responses. Discuss Mustafa's chances of winning the competition.